sempé

Mixed Messages

Φ

Oh, what a wonderful, marvellous day we're going to have together – my dear friend Solitude and I!

*Yes, I often ask myself the same question; what kind of society
are we leaving to our children?*

Boldly tumbling down the steep slopes of Mount Gravillac and falling to the limestone plateaux of the Cretaceous era, this water re-emerges in the silt of the Malzac springs, carpeted as they are with fine sand, and then, invigorated by its contact with ferruginous sandstone, casts itself into the Arpemont valley where it finally comes to rest, retaining all its mineral goodness.

I truly pity you, Martha! You have never known happiness. Real, true happiness!
The kind that sets your heart racing, prevents you from breathing properly, rules out any
kind of rational thought, ties your stomach in knots, makes you lose your appetite, sleep,
your friends and your family, and inexorably grinds you down.

Time has passed, I have rebuilt my life, but I have never forgotten you, Roberto.

*There's a thought that often crosses my mind: suppose something happened to me,
would my family and friends need psychological counselling?*

You have reached Dr Grunstein's consulting rooms.
If you are undergoing analysis, press 2.
If you want to undergo analysis, press 2 and then the star key.
If you have already begun analysis elsewhere, press 2 and then the hash key.
If you have interrupted your analysis because you have been hospitalized,
press 3 and then the hash key.
If you are going away, press 3, then the hash key and then 4.
If you are calling for no particular reason, press 4 and then the star key.
If you want to begin a new analysis, press 5, then the star key and then 6.
Otherwise, please hang up.

*I saw a terrible accident just now: a man crossing the road and talking on his mobile was knocked down
by a motorist who was using his mobile too. By the time the ambulance arrived it was too late.
Everyone was horrified. Everything stopped. Then we heard a mobile ringing in someone's pocket, a few
notes of Mozart, or something, and life returned to normal.*

Where are you? Hello, where are you? Where are you? … Hello, where are you? Hello, where are you?

Martha? Suzanne here. I'm in Our Lady of the Redemption. Would you like me to ask for anything for you too?

I spent the whole service in a strange state, hovering a few centimetres above the ground.
When it was over I came back down to earth, treading on my sister's left foot and slightly
spraining my ankle. Our next step, if I may put it that way, is to get a medical certificate
and come back to see you, so that we can all discuss the best way to proceed
as a consequence of this unusual incident.

How nice of you to come in your cassock, Father!

And this year I decided to go on pilgrimage to Santiago de Compostela. It's tough at first. Both body and spirit rebel, but then, after a few days, a kind of serenity comes over you. Many of your prejudices and assumptions simply fade away. You are overcome by a great sense of wisdom, and when I reached the Châteauroux area, and passed a railway station, it seemed perfectly natural for me to go and join Solange and the kids at Le Touquet.

1.

2.

3.

4.

5.

6.

7.

Wedded bliss really suits you.

I recommend the caprice of the season, the chef's surprise salad or the tarantella of tartlets served with wild thyme and heartsease dressing.

How much is that one?

She started by phoning me ten times a day. "I love you," she said. Then she took to calling once a day. "I love you very much," she said. Now I get a call once every two weeks, saying, "I love you very very very much," but I'm an optimist, I keep reminding myself of Adamson's theory that intensity grows greater as frequency grows less.

Conjuges debent jurare fidelitatem *(those joined in matrimony must swear fidelity)* aeternam
(which we might roughly translate today as: there is no such thing as a risk-free situation).

1.

2.

5.

6.

9.

10.

3.

4.

7.

8.

11.

12.

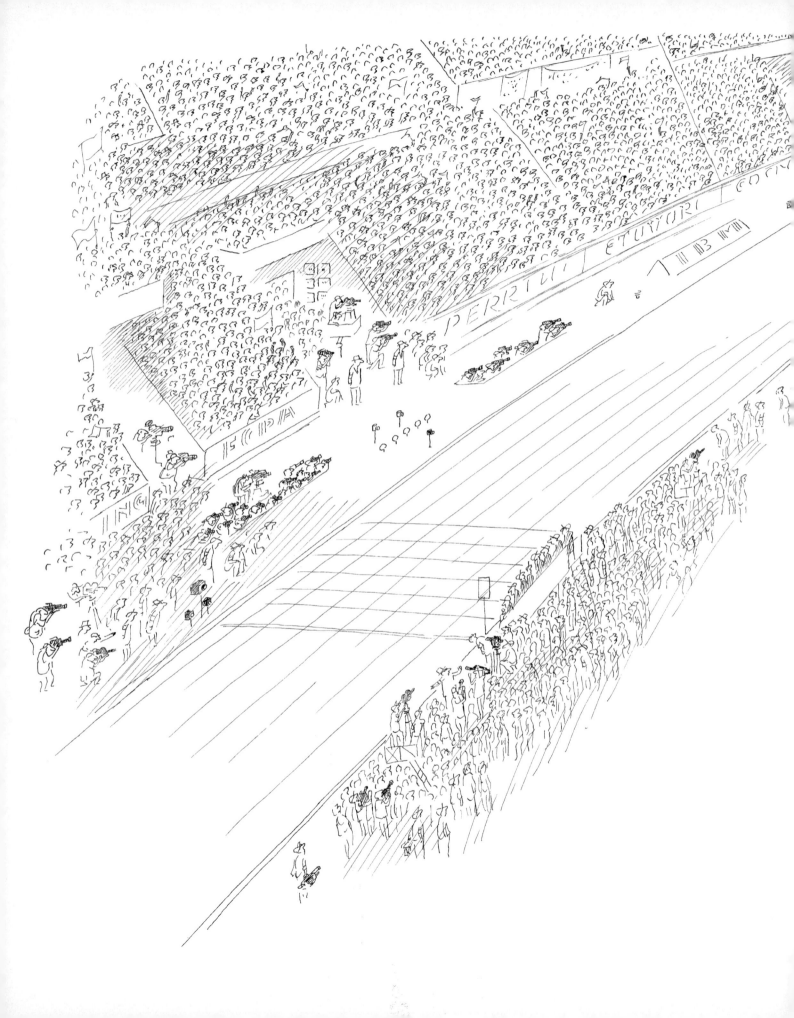

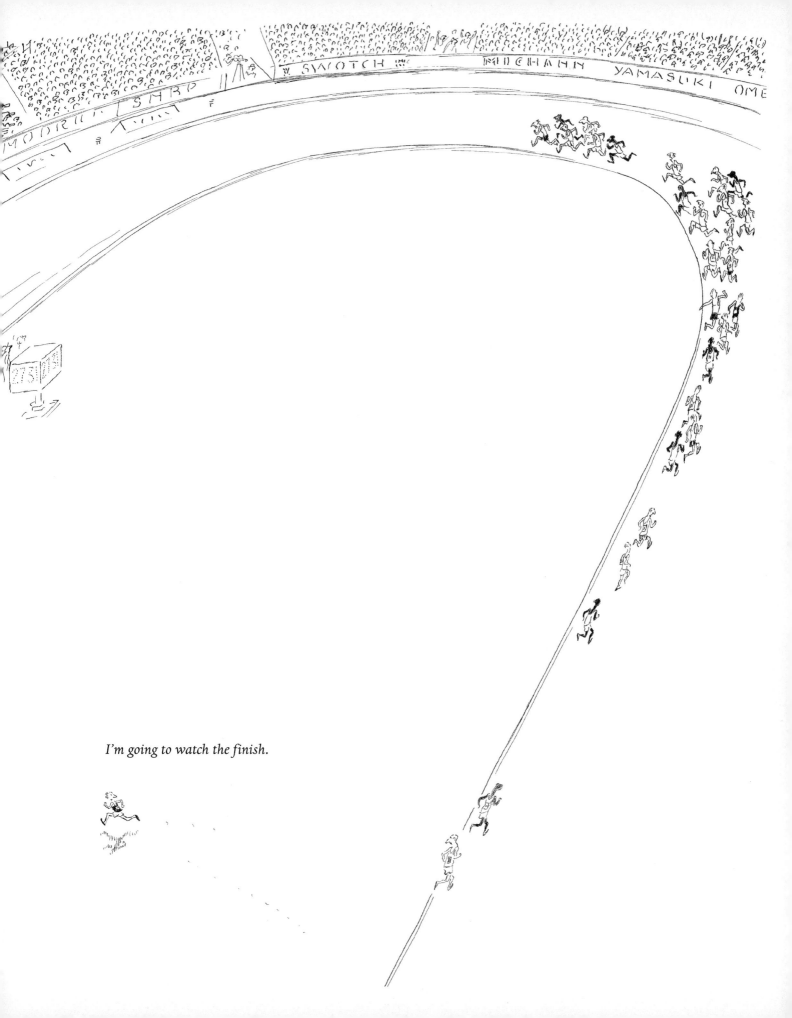

I'm going to watch the finish.

I've resoled your shoes, Elizabeth. In doing so I noticed that you put too much weight on the outside of your right heel, which in the long run will cause dislocation of the hip and be bad for your lumbar and above all your cervical vertebrae, causing migraines which will have an adverse effect on your temperament (and I should know). I have therefore corrected the balance of your shoe (we'll see about correcting your gait later), and I hope that will allow us to resume our relationship on a better footing.

He never says, "You look beautiful," he says, "You don't look bad today."
And he never tells me, "That was a delicious dinner you cooked," he says, "Your cooking
is all right." The fact is, I feel like telling him, "I'm leaving," but I say,
"I really don't know why I bother to stay."

At this moment in time we are fully booked.

All these years I've lived surrounded by perfect breasts, figures and legs. Perfection is inhuman, no one can live with it. Without you, Miss Yvonne, I could never have survived. Today, on the eve of my retirement, I wanted to thank you. I kept ringing for you to open your window so that despite your sour, grumpy look, or perhaps because of it, I could catch a glimpse of that residue of humanity which enabled me to carry out my duties.

The third clarinettist is unwell. He has been replaced by Frederick Lelièvre, an experienced instrumentalist with a deep and convincing tone in the bass register, and what is certainly a brilliant vibrato in the higher register, although it is a little too showy for my taste and too obviously designed to appeal to the common herd.

I really enjoy discussing the theatre with you. I completely agree: above all, drama is the art of the ephemeral.
So now I don't feel so bad about telling you that I'm giving the part you played this evening to Bouchart instead.

He started out with a donkey (me). We delivered cheeses in the local villages. We worked hard, but he was happy as a sandboy. Then, little by little, it became a business. Eighty employees including his ambitious son-in-law. His wife gives garden parties. Exhausted, he took to golf. The other evening, quite late, I put my head through his office window. He was hunched over his computer. I wanted to tell him, "Let's go back to the old days when you were so happy! Your faithful old Kiki (me again) is still here." He nearly jumped out of his skin and went for me with his golf club. I know a bray may sound like mocking laughter or an alarming sob, but all the same I can't help thinking communication is very difficult.

No, no! They said no!

I'm fine. But I'd be even better if I knew you were feeling fine. If I ask you of course you'll tell me you're fine.
But since I don't know if you tell me what you're really thinking, I'm not as fine as I might be.

Very good. Now paint another.

*Yes, I have several things on the boil at the moment: a Chateaubriand – a biography of him,
I mean; an essay on nuclear power and an avant-garde novel.*

In January we kill a pig, and then we have ham, sausages, pâtés, etc.
Everyone's well stocked up for the year. Everyone's happy. Except the pigs.

I'm so glad to see you again. Remember that unhappy love affair I told you about last year,
the one that spoilt part of your holiday – no, don't deny it, I know it did! Well,
it was absolutely nothing compared to what I'm going through now!

As soon as I knew you were in these parts I told myself I must pay a formal visit.

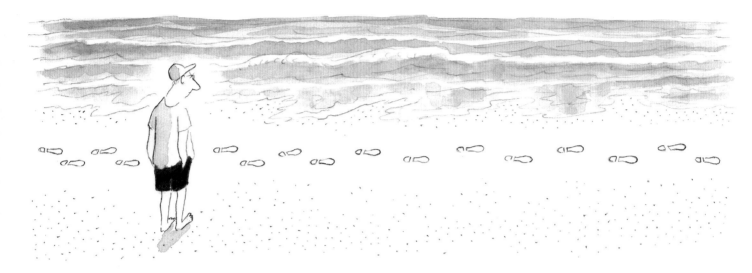

1.

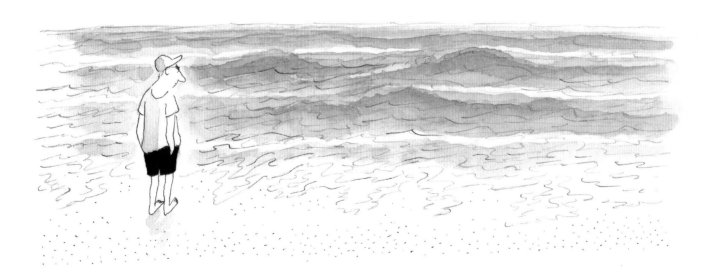

2.

3.

Ladies and gentlemen, we ask you to switch off your mobile phones so that we can all enjoy the sunset.

Life never ceases to surprise me: the day you caught that huge pike, and then the fabulous trout a week later,
I confess I envied your delight and the pride of your nearest and dearest. I was wrong to envy you. You have become
nervy and irritable. But I do understand: the little minnows you've been catching ever since must be a severe
disappointment. I, on the other hand, feel that my loved ones rest easy in the knowledge that there will always be
something for a fry-up – not a large catch, maybe, but reliable and ultimately reassuring.

*Nothing ever changes: as a kid I was terrified when darkness fell and I went to fetch milk from the farm.
I thought wolves or monsters were waiting to jump out at me. These days, when the time for the TV news
approaches, I tell myself the Dow Jones or the FTSE 100 are going to rip me to shreds.*

We must study our accommodation, our opportunities for communication and the co-ordination of our activities, in short, logistics.
But first and most important, we must make up our minds to agree on the subject of sex tourism.

What bothers me is the way we're racing at breakneck speed towards world government.

As fellow musicians, many things remind us both of our musical scores. Standing here every morning, I imagine notes over there. Notes by Mozart, Schubert, Beethoven ... whereas you, my dear Paul, I can sense beside me mentally scribbling down Stravinsky, Stockhausen or (it's much the same thing to me) a polka. And so, dear Paul, in the name of freedom of expression, I have finally got the management of the College of Music to let you begin your classes an hour earlier.

When you pray you ask for something, when I pray I ask for you not to ask me for anything.

Yes, it's a lot of money, but it's not expensive.

Personally I'd never have the patience.

I like it when he loses his temper.

It's a never-ending flow of inspiration.

*I want a book on geopolitics that is clearly aimed at a particular audience and specific
enough for me to apply some of its principles to my immediate surroundings.*

And then, in the middle of the second chapter, I realized that my characters were beginning to develop a life of their own, a life that, in a way, they were imposing on me, so that towards the end, from the fifth and sixth chapters onwards, they impelled me, you might say they positively forced me, to change publishers.

Bernard, I must let you know about the end of a friendship: ours. Yesterday you told me that you felt you had been overtaken. I asked sympathetically: "Overtaken by what?" You told me: "By everything. Life, people." In friendly tones, I said: "What, even by me?" To which you replied: "By you? Why on earth would I feel overtaken by you? Goodness me, no, not in the least!"

94

I know it's all long ago, Clothilde, but I would really like to return to the subject
of this so-called dark side of mine that scared you away. If we could talk about this,
you may discover that my dark side could have been a source of joy and delight to you.

The first part of my book therapeutically allowed me to express my sense of guilt for the incestuous relationship into which my father forced me. But it was when I came to write the second part (in which I discover that he is having the same relationship with my sister) that I understood my subconscious motivation for writing the book in the first place. We have to ask ourselves: "What on earth did he see in her?"

When I come to a place like this I sense that I am really myself. I talk to people, I feel a different person in every conversation. I try to discover my true self, but I am no longer the man I was. Then I get home (late). Claire's voice calls to me from the bedroom, crossly: "Is that you?" I tell her it is, and I feel reassured.

When everyone is talking nonsense, spying on you, keeping a close watch on your ideas so as
to distort them later, you can't think how restful it is to talk to someone who doesn't answer,
may not even see you, and probably doesn't hear you either.

I started out with STOFAT, which merged with SPOFI to become STOCAFIT. Then I was appointed to manage a branch called SUFITA which expanded and became POFITECH. You could say I've had a brilliant career. But sometimes I think: oh, PHOOEY.

Phaidon Press Limited
Regent's Wharf
All Saints Street
London N1 9PA

Phaidon Press Inc.
180 Varick Street
New York, NY 10014

www.phaidon.com

English Edition © 2006 Phaidon Press Ltd
First published in French as
Multiples Intentions by Éditions Denoël
© 2003 Sempé and Éditions Denoël

ISBN 0 7148 4543 4

A CIP catalogue record for this book is
available from the British Library.

Translated by Anthea Bell
Designed by James Cartledge and
Phil Evans of etal-design
Printed in China